EXPERIENCE
GOD'S PRESENCE

An Experience like no other....

EXPERIENCE GOD'S PRESENCE

You become what you behold...
Secrets of the Soul....

MELISSA LANZA

Hurricane Sandy Survivor

TATE PUBLISHING
AND ENTERPRISES, LLC

Experience God's Presence
Copyright © 2014 by Melissa Lanza. All rights reserved.

No part of this publication may be reproduced, stored in a retrieval system or transmitted in any way by any means, electronic, mechanical, photocopy, recording or otherwise without the prior permission of the author except as provided by USA copyright law.

This book is designed to provide accurate and authoritative information with regard to the subject matter covered. This information is given with the understanding that neither the author nor Tate Publishing, LLC is engaged in rendering legal, professional advice. Since the details of your situation are fact dependent, you should additionally seek the services of a competent professional.

The opinions expressed by the author are not necessarily those of Tate Publishing, LLC.

Published by Tate Publishing & Enterprises, LLC
127 E. Trade Center Terrace | Mustang, Oklahoma 73064 USA
1.888.361.9473 | www.tatepublishing.com

Tate Publishing is committed to excellence in the publishing industry. The company reflects the philosophy established by the founders, based on Psalm 68:11,
"The Lord gave the word and great was the company of those who published it."

Book design copyright © 2014 by Tate Publishing, LLC. All rights reserved.
Cover design by Gian Philipp Rufin
Interior design by Mary Jean Archival
Photos taken by Melissa Lanza
Book cover taken by Melissa Lanza
All interior photos taken by Melissa Lanza, except on page 10.

Published in the United States of America

ISBN: 978-1-63367-415-8
Religion / Christian Life / Inspirational / Spirituality
14.10.10

I dedicate this book to God.

In loving memory of Concetta and Michael Lanza.
In grateful appreciation to my dad, mom,
aunt Phyllis, and the entire Lanza family.
Thank you to all my friends, Daughters
of Divine Charity, sisters who taught me,
especially Sister Denise and Sister Mary.
Love to Dana and Sean Dolan,
and godchildren, C. J. and Michael.
Special remembrance to the late Fr. John King, SJ.
Special acknowledgment to St. Clare's Prayer Group.
May this book bless all of you and be used
to give glory and honor to God forever!

Contents

Introduction 9
I Am Thirsty. Can You Give Me a Drink? 13
God the Initiator 15
God the Lover of All Souls 15
Preparation of Our Hearts 19
Listening 21
Waiting 27
Prayer 33
Attitudes of the Heart 37
The Journey 39
Experience God's Presence 41
In My Presence: The Secret Place of His Presence 97

Ministering to the Lord	105
Preserving Our Faith: How to Protect Yourself from Evil	109
Rewards	115
The Call of the Great Commission	121

Introduction

Many books have been written and continue to be written about God and prayer. This book will teach a person how to connect, encounter, and experience God inside the center of oneself, to experience God's presence inside one's own heart. What is God's presence like? How do we get that water so that we will never be thirsty again? What is that water mentioned in the Bible about the woman at the well?

There is that sacred space inside every human being that longs for the Divine, the spiritual part of our beings. It is the space where the human and divine meet. The focal point where the soul and Divine become one, an amazing secret of the soul. You become what you behold, an experience like no other.

IN MY PRESENCE

You do not realize that you would have broken down under the weight of your cares but for the renewing time with Me. It is not what I say; it is I, Myself. It is not the hearing Me so much as the being *In My Presence*. The strengthening and curative powers of this you cannot know. Such knowledge is beyond your human reckoning. This would cure the poor sick world, if every day, each soul, or group of souls, waited before Me. Remember, that you must never fail to keep this time apart with Me. Gradually you will be transformed, physically, mentally, spiritually, into *my* likeness. All who see you, or contact with you will be, by this intercourse with you, brought near to Me, and gradually the influence will spread. You are making one spot of earth a Holy Place, and though you must work and spend yourself ceaselessly, because that is for the present your appointed task, yet the greatest work either of you can do, and are doing, is done in this time apart with Me. Are you understanding that? Do you know that every thought, every activity, every prayer, every longing of the day is gathered up and offered to Me, now?

Oh! Joy that I am with you. For this I came to earth, to lead man back to spirit-converse with his God (AJ Russell Ed. *God Calling*. London: Arthur James Limited 1953).

Someone that I know read the first book I wrote, In My Presence. She was away on vacation reading it on the beach. After she closed the book, she looked up in the sky and saw this:

She stated that she experienced God's presence. In these pages, you will read some of the experiences other people have had of God's presence. This book will teach you how to have this depth of love, joy, peace, unveiling mystery, and excitement in your everyday life—a relationship, an experience truly like no other. See the desert bloom in your own life and live life fully alive with the Resurrection Power that has been given to us here and now, truly living life to the fullest so that we will never be thirsty again.

I Am Thirsty. Can You Give Me a Drink?

In the book of John, it states that "whoever drinks the water I give him will never thirst. The water I give him will become in him a spring of water welling up to eternal life." It states in the scripture that the time is coming when the true worshipers will worship the Father in spirit and in truth, for they are the kind of worshipers the Father seeks. God is spirit and His worshipers must worship in spirit and in truth.

What is this thirst? Who is thirsty? Why? How can this thirst be quenched? What is this water that quenches all thirst and how does one obtain this water? God created man. Our souls have been created by God. God desires to have a personal relationship with each one of us. There is a desire and a thirst inside the center of each person that desires God. We have to choose in our free will to desire God. As you know, man has searched in different ways to fill this void we were born with through drugs, sex, alcohol, rock 'n' roll, money, power, success, and control. Some people have chosen not to have God fill their void. Sometimes people choose to be gamblers, alcoholics, criminals, and sex offenders, or to be addicted to food and shopping. There is a desire for man to be fulfilled. Each person searches in different ways. Our hearts are restless until they rest in God. To be totally possessed by God and to find God inside the deepest center of oneself, in our hearts, is where the soul feels the presence of God. This is the living water where all thirst is totally quenched once the soul is touched by God inside our own hearts.

On a human level, our bodies desire great things, like desiring the best brand names in the material world. Our hearts desire to love and be loved. We crave the touch of another human being. We seek fulfillment but are often left empty and insatiable. Wealth is not evil in and of itself, but if it becomes a god in our lives, it is wrong. If we are willing to pay the high prices for name brands such as Coach, Fendi, or Louis Vuitton, how much are we willing to strive in our spiritual lives and to have that close union with our God? How much more we can have in our lives if we just craved to be touched by both God and man?

God the Initiator
God the Lover of All Souls

The Bible states that we are to love the Lord our God with all our heart, mind, will, and soul. The greatest commandment is love. John 15:16 (Life Application Study Bible, New International Version Copyright) states, "You did not choose Me, but I chose you and appointed you to go and bear fruit and that your fruit should remain." And in Revelation 3:20, "Behold, I stand at the door and knock. If anyone hears My voice and opens the door, I will come in to him and dine with him and he with Me." For it is God who works in you both to will and to do for His good pleasure (Phil. 2:13). By this we know love because He laid down His life for us (John 3:16). All things have been delivered to me by my Father, and no one knows who the Son is except the Father, and who the Father is except the Son, and the one to whom the Son wills to reveal Him (Luke 10:22).

These are examples of how God pursues a love relationship and how He is the Initiator. We are to know, worship, and love God. Jesus said in John 14:21, "He who has My commandments and keeps them, it is he who loves Me. He who loves Me will be loved by My Father, and I will love him and manifest

Myself to him. If you want God to reveal Himself to you, you must love and obey Him."

In a book called *Experiencing God* by Henry T. Blackaby and Claude V. King, it is mentioned that God reveals Himself with a purpose. He created you for a relationship with Himself. When He reveals Himself to you, He is allowing you to come to know Him by experience. This revelation is an expression of God's love for you. This experience is a result of being *in His presence.* If you experience God's comfort during a time of grief, you could relate to God as the comforter in sorrow. You come to know God when He reveals Himself to you. You come to know Him as you experience Him. This encounter becomes personal and is a direct result of spending time in God's presence.

To call on God's name is to seek His presence. God's name is worthy of our praise. Acknowledging God's name amounts to recognizing God for who He is. Calling on His name indicates you are seeking His presence. God's names in Scripture can become a call to worship. His name represents His presence. The names of God in Scripture reveal something of His nature, activity, or character. You come to know God by experience at His initiative as He reveals Himself to you. Some of the names include the following: my witness (Job 16:19), bread of life (John 6:35), comforter in sorrow (Jer. 8:18), my hope (Psalm 77:5), wonderful counselor (Isaiah 9:6), defender of widows (Psalm 68:5), my friend (Job 16:20), my hiding place (Psalm 32:7), lord of Lords (1 Tim. 6:15), refuge and strength (Psalm 46:1), and good teacher (Mark 10:17).

Preparation of Our Hearts

Part of being able to enter into the presence of God is to prepare our hearts to receive Him. There are practical things one needs to do before hand. Just like in human relationships, for example in a marriage, the stage needs to be set in order for one to enter into the intimacy of one's marriage vows. The relationship requires love and attention to it.

In relating with God, the first priority is to set aside a certain time of the day or night when one can be together with God, free of distractions. Our schedules are very busy with school, work, raising a family, or providing care for loved ones. The commitment of a specific time and being consistent and faithful every day is very important. The greatest temptation is to stop doing this by making excuses about how busy we are or by stopping completely if we feel we are wasting time or we think nothing is happening. Setting time and making a faithful commitment to spending time with God is essential.

The environment should be quiet and peaceful. Our hearts need to be silent. Initially, many thoughts will enter the mind once one tries to be silent. Or we could make the most noise and drop things or trip into things as soon as one tries to be still and silent. Or just as one tries to do this, another distraction will come—the phone will ring or we will remember that we forgot to do something. Did I lock the house, turn the gas off? Or what will I decide to make for dinner? Did I defrost the steak? Did I forget to buy milk? Being silent is so foreign in our society. If it is too quiet in a house, the TV, radio, iPod, or computer will be usually turned on. Silence can be very uncomfortable for some people. For us to face ourselves, we have to look at our thoughts and what we are thinking. Some thoughts can be good and some thoughts can be bad. We may have a memory entering our mind that could be pleasant or painful. This is okay, just be silent and let thoughts, distractions, memories, and ideas just pass the same way the clouds pass by in the sky. The goal is to let them pass and become like a blank computer screen before God. When this happens, our hearts are starting to empty, and we can then start the next step.

Listening

As we start to settle down inwardly and we become like a blank computer screen before God, then we can start to listen internally to the deep voice within us. It is a still small voice. How does one listen? Once the time is scheduled and our hearts are silent, we can listen just like the people did in Biblical times. Here are some examples from Scripture:

In the book of 1 Kings 19: 10–18, the Lord appeared to Elijah. And the word of the Lord came to him, "What are you doing here, Elijah?" He replied, "I have been very zealous for the Lord God Almighty. The Israelites have rejected your covenant, broken down your altars, and put your prophets to death with the sword. I am the only one left, and now they are trying to kill me too." The Lord said, "Go out and stand on the mountain in the presence of the Lord, for the Lord is about to pass by." Then a great and powerful wind tore the mountains apart and shattered the rocks before the Lord, but the Lord was not in the wind. After the wind there was an earthquake, but the Lord was not in the earthquake. After the earthquake came a fire, but the Lord was not in the fire. And after the fire came a gentle whisper. When Elijah heard it, he pulled back his cloak over his face and went out and stood at the mouth of the cave. Then a voice said to him, "What are you doing here, Elijah?" He replied, "I have been very zealous for the Lord God Almighty. The Israelites have rejected your covenant, broken down your altars, and put your prophets to death with the sword. I am the only one left, and now they are trying to kill me too." The Lord said to him, "Go back the way you came, and go to the desert of Damascus. When you get there, anoint Hazel king over Aram. Also, anoint Jehu son of Nimshi king over Israel, and anoint Elisha son of Shaphat from Abel Meholah to succeed you as prophet. Jehu will put to death any who escape the sword of Hazael, and Elisha will put to death any who escape the sword of Jehu. Yet I reserve seven thousand in Israel all whose knees have not bowed down to Baal and all whose mouths have not kissed him."

Another example in the Bible is from the book of Deuteronomy 4:33–38:

> Has any other person heard the voice of God speaking out of fire, as you have, and lived? Has any god ever tried to take for himself one nation out of another nation, by testings, by miraculous signs and wonders,

by war, by a mighty hand and an outstretched arm, or by great and awesome deeds, like all the things the Lord your God did for you in Egypt before your very eyes? (Please note this book is focusing on God's relationship with Moses.) You were shown these things so that you might know that the Lord is God; besides him there is no other. From heaven he made you hear his voice to discipline you. On earth he showed you his great fire, and you heard his words from out of the fire. Because he loved your forefathers and chose their descendants after them, he brought you out of Egypt by his Presence and his great strength, to drive out before you nations greater and stronger than you and to bring you into their land to give it to you for your inheritance, as it is today.

In the book of Deuteronomy 5:22–32, another example is shown about listening to God and hearing his voice;

These are the commandments the Lord proclaimed in a loud voice to your whole assembly there on the mountain from out of the fire, the cloud and the deep darkness; and he added nothing more. Then he wrote them on two stone tablets and gave them to me.

When you heard the voice out of the darkness, while the mountain was ablaze with fire, all the leading men of your tribes and your elders came to me. And you said, "The Lord our God has shown us his glory and his majesty, and we have heard his voice from the fire. Today we have seen that a man can live even if God speaks with him. But now, why should we die? This great fire will consume us, and we will die if we hear the voice of the Lord our God any longer. For what mortal man has ever heard the voice of the living God speaking out of fire, as we have, and survived? Go near and listen to all that the Lord our God says. Then tell us whatever the Lord our God tells you. We will listen and obey." The Lord heard you when you spoke to me and the Lord said to me, "I have heard what this people said to you. Everything they said was good. Oh, that their hearts would be inclined to fear me and keep my commands always, so that it might go well with them and their children forever! "Go; tell them to return to their tents. But you stay here with me so that I may give you all the commands, decrees and laws you are to teach them to follow in the land I am giving them to possess." So be careful to do what the Lord your God has commanded you; do not turn aside to the right or to the left. Walk in all the way that the Lord your God has commanded you, so that you may live and prosper and prolong your days in the land that you will possess.

We see how the Bible gives examples in the lives of the people of what it means to listen. How do we listen now to God in this century? For me, listening to God happened when I received the call to become a nurse. I looked at the gifts God gave me and listened to the desires of my heart and figured out through listening if nursing would be a good fit for my career. A synchronization of discovering who I am as a person, what talents God had given me, and was this the right decision for me. When I listened inwardly to all this, I was able to figure it out. When I discussed this with others, people agreed and confirmed my gifts and thought it fit right with who I was as a person.

A friend of mine shared the following. She decided to get married by listening to her own heart and to others. First, she had said yes to go on the first date. Through the dating process, and over time, she decided to marry him. Making her decision involved listening and being inwardly attuned to the desires of her heart, knowing who she was as a person with all her strengths and weaknesses, and learning who her future husband was. Did they love each other enough? Were they compatible? The listening process was crucial to the matter of two hearts deciding to marry.

Someone else shared with me about how he became a priest and someone else who decided to become a sister in a religious community. The process was similar—the idea of listening to one's heart and being called by God and sensitive to the inner workings of one's heart, talents, and gifts. Listening helps one to make important decisions in one's life. It involves a position of one's heart, to be still and know that He is God, to listen to the inner gut, inner voice inside us. Sometimes we doubt ourselves and do not always listen to our gut or our feelings. It is the voice of our conscience.

Waiting

Part of being able to be in the presence of God is to prepare our hearts through waiting. Waiting is very important. To wait in silence combines the steps at the same time with setting the time, listening, and now waiting. Waiting is a very difficult thing to do, and it is countercultural. We have instant mashed potatoes, instant coffee, microwaves heat up in thirty seconds to minutes, computers e-mail in millionths of a second, and fast-food restaurants. For the most part, waiting is becoming as extinct as the dinosaurs. However, it is an essential ingredient to our spiritual lives in obtaining this intimacy with God that I am writing about. The biggest temptation one can face is to give up trying to wait on the Lord especially when one perceives that nothing is happening at all. This is when I have to remind myself how long it takes when a seed is planted in the dark soil buried in the earth. Once it is planted, the farmer must wait for it to grow into a crop. The process is slow, and all we can do is hurry up and wait. Don't give up. Wait on the Lord. Easier said than done. How does one wait on the Lord? Let us examine how we do this according to the Bible.

Waiting on the Lord develops absolute dependence on Him. Your waiting on Him assures that you will act on His timing and not your own (Blackby and King, 1994). The book of Isaiah 40:31 says that those who wait on the Lord shall renew their strength, they shall mount up with wings like eagles, they shall run, and not be weary and they shall walk and not faint. Psalm 33:26 says, "Our soul waits for the Lord. He is our help and our shield." Psalm 37:34 states, "Wait on the Lord, and keep His way and He shall exalt you to inherit the land." Psalm 38:15 states, "For in You, O Lord I hope, You will hear, O Lord my God. Psalm 5:3 states, "My voice you shall hear in the morning, O Lord, in the morning I will direct it to You and I will look up."

Waiting on the Lord is active. It is not a passive, inactive activity. While you are waiting on Him, you will be praying with a passion to know Him, His purposes and His ways. You will be watching circumstances and asking God to interpret them by revealing to you His perspective. As you wait on the Lord, you will be asking, seeking, and knocking. "Ask, and it will be given to you, seek, and you will find, knock, and the door will be opened to you. For everyone who asks receives, and he who seeks finds and to him who knocks the door will be opened" (Matthew 7:7–8).

In waiting, you are shifting the responsibilities of the outcome to God where it belongs. Then when God gives you specific guidance, he will do through you in more days and weeks than you could ever accomplish in years of labor. Waiting on Him is always worth the wait. His timing and His ways are always right. You must depend on Him to guide you in His way and in His timing to accomplish His purpose.

When speaking with others about waiting, others have shared with me their experiences.

One person who wishes to remain unknown for purposes of this book told me that waiting helped them to increase their faith, and it humbled them to become totally dependent on God alone. It helped them to not insist on doing things their own way. Waiting helps to remind me she stated to live by faith trusting the Holy Spirit within us every moment of every day to conform us to become the likeness of God's Son Jesus Christ.

For myself, waiting on God has been a very hard experience for me. I had to unlearn everything I was taught as a child. For example, as a child I was taught to work hard, strive for excellence, do your very best, set goals, and pursue them with diligence and determination. These are great ideals to have, and they are necessary when remaining gainfully employed. However, it can deceive us by suggesting our salvation lies in them, meaning it leads us to believe that we have to earn our way to Heaven. It whispers to the ego, "You have all the time that it takes to be successful." If we pay attention strictly to this idea, it creates an idol of self-effort. It can derail us from our pursuit of holiness and union with God. Waiting has taught me to eliminate this idol in my life. It has taught me to rely on His grace, and it has taught me to see how dependent I am on Him alone for victorious living. Waiting stretches my heart to be more open to receive God and to experience His love and presence in my life. Waiting is also His way of achieving other purposes in our lives. He wants His grace and goodness to shine through us and for others to see His handiwork in us, to shine through us.

A Presbyterian minister was quoted in an interview saying, "The assumption of spirituality is that always God is doing something before I know it. So the task is not to get God to do something before I know it or to get God to do something I think needs to be done, but to become aware of what God is doing so that I can respond to it, participate, and take delight in it." This is the motivation behind waiting prayer. We place ourselves in the postures of the heart, in the stillness that enables us to become aware of what God is doing so that we can gradually say yes to it with our whole being.

Another young forty-three-year-old woman shared her experience. She is a career woman who excelled in the corporate world and reached the top rung in her corporation. She achieved this and started to feel burnt out. She started to experience an internal crisis, questioned how she was living her life, started doubting herself, her relationships, and commitments. Felt like, why bother? She took time and went on vacation to Maine. She asked God to change things in her life, as she walked in the country while on vacation. She noticed a spider web that hung between two trees. The spider was still in the midst of spinning it. She stopped and watched it. It occurred to her that she never did anything so irrelevant like this in her life. She realized that waiting always feels irrelevant in the beginning. Yet she sat down on a stump and watched the spider. The most beautiful thing happened. She realized this is the way you are supposed to pray. Just be quiet and still so that you can begin to see the thing God is already weaving. There was silence between God and herself. Something like this changed her. She realized how God strews paths with little webs of grace that pulled her into the prayer of waiting into healing and rebirth (reference used: *When the Heart Waits* by Sue Monk Kidd).

This became a prayer of concentrated stillness where we become the cocoon. When our hearts, body, mind, spirit become still, it creates the waiting season in which we become able to commune with our depths and begin to recover what is lost, heal what is wounded, and become who we truly are.

I had this kind of experience when I lost my house to Hurricane Sandy. The hurricane caused me to face my brokenness, my nothingness. I had nothing to give God or anyone. I lost everything, and all I could do was receive. I had to rely on others to give me shelter, food, clothing, etc. I was stripped down to faith, hope, and love. I had my relationships with God and others. It was a time of chaos in my life. Everything was upside down. In a flash, my life changed, and I was homeless.

I had to tap into my soul for what was left. I was still able to give love and receive love, still able to pray for others to be a lover of God and His people, to find God in the garbage and rubble. My garbage brought out to the curb in front of the house with everyone else on the block, still being loved with my brokenness, disaster number from FEMA, being naked, vulnerable and alone. Like having to totally trust, let go and surrender, to surrender and put everything in His hands. Thought I did this already. Never like this now. In my brokenness, my situation, I was one hot mess. Nothing stopped God. Years and years of waiting on God in a flash of time, God showed me something beautiful. He made His home in my heart. It was as if three people moved inside of me: Father, Son, and Holy Spirit. It was so different now. We are taught that this happens to us when we are baptized. We believe this happens through our faith by believing. Never, not until now it was in a flash as fast as one can put on a light switch; one moment in time my heart knew and experienced it in the depths of my soul. The Father, Son, and Holy Spirit let me know they were there—an experience like no other. They moved into my heart, and nothing has been the same since. Waiting… waiting… waiting… never experienced anything like this before—a piece of Heaven on Earth. It was an experience of true union with God, one with God.

Prayer

Spend time walking and talking with God. Focus your thoughts on your love of God; praise Him for His love and mercy. Take time to worship and adore Him. Then just spend time with Him. Talk to Him and listen to what He may say to you. Listen in silence after reflecting on your feelings. Try to write down in a journal what you have just heard as you listened to God in prayer. Do this every day; sit in His presence. How does a person sit in His presence?

Examples for this type of prayer are found in the Bible. The book of Matthew 26:36–45 states that Jesus went with His disciples to a place called Gethsemane, and He said to them, "Sit here and wait while I pray." He took Peter and the two sons of Zebedee along with Him, and He began to be sorrowful and troubled. Then He said to them, "My soul is overwhelmed with sorrow to the point of death. Stay here and keep watch with Me." This is an example of waiting that was mentioned in the previous chapter. Going a little farther, He fell with his face to the ground and prayed, "My Father, if it is possible, may this cup be taken from me. Yet not as I will, but as You will." Then He returned to his disciples and found them sleeping. "Could you men not keep watch with Me for one hour?" He asked Peter. "Watch and pray so that you will not fall into temptation. The spirit is willing, but the flesh is weak." He went away a second time and prayed, "My Father, if it is not possible for this cup to be taken away unless I drink it, may Your will be done." When He came back, he again found them sleeping, because their eyes were heavy. So He left them and went away once more and prayed the third time, saying the same thing. Then He returned to the disciples and said to them, "Are you still sleeping and resting? Look, the hour is near, and the Son of Man is betrayed into the hands of sinners. Rise, let us go! Here comes My betrayer!"

In Matthew 6: 5–14, Jesus teaches us how to pray. "And when you pray, do not be like the hypocrites, for they love to pray standing in the synagogues and on the street corners to be seen by men. I tell you the truth; they have received their reward in full. But when you pray, go into your room, close the door and pray to your Father, who is unseen. Then your Father, who sees what is done in secret, will reward you. And when you pray, do not keep on babbling like pagans, for they think they will be heard because of their many words. Do not be like them, for your Father knows what you need before you ask him. This, then, is how you should pray: Our Father in heaven, hallowed be Your name, Your kingdom come, Your will be done on earth as it is in heaven. Give us today our daily bread. Forgive us our debts, as we also have forgiven our debtors. And lead us not into temptation, but deliver us from the evil one. For if you forgive men when they sin against you, your heavenly Father will also forgive you. But if you do not forgive men their sins, your Father will not forgive your sins."

In summary, Jesus was setting up a way to relate and pray to God. One thinks of one word—ACTS. The prayer contains adoration and praise. "Hallowed be thy name" means how great God is. Contrition involves expressing sorrow and seeking forgiveness of our sins towards others, ourselves, and God. Thanksgiving is to express gratitude in our hearts to God and others for the blessings we receive. Supplication is asking for our needs to be met and asking for God's will to be done in our lives.

It is also important to see an example from Jesus's life in how He needed to spend time alone with God and so do we. The book of Mark 6:12–16 states that one of those days, Jesus went out to a mountainside to pray and spent the night praying to God. When morning came, he called his disciples to him and chose the twelve of them, whom he also designated apostles: Simon (whom he named Peter); his brother Andrew; James; John; Philip; Bartholomew; Matthew; Thomas; James, son of Alphaeus; Simon, who was called the Zealot; Judas, son of James; and Judas Iscariot, who became a traitor.

Jesus also spent time alone with His Father when He wept over Jerusalem. These are examples of the way Jesus prayed when He lived on this earth. He is our model of how we are supposed to live our lives.

Some people pray by reading the Scriptures and meditating on them. Others will play CDs with Christian music on them. Some people will sing and worship, and others will just be still and listen to the music and pray. Other people will take a walk in a park, beach, mountains, desert, and nature scenes near a waterfall, lake, and ocean and spend time in prayer with God. Whatever way is fine as long as a soul encounters God and has intimacy with God. Time with God enriches and deepens the relationship. The more you know Him and experience His love, the more you will love Him. Then you will want that time alone with Him because you love Him, enjoy His fellowship, and will just want to be with Him. One will love God for who He is. The more one loves Him the more one wants to do His will and please Him.

Attitudes of the Heart

After one prays every day, the heart starts to change. The relationship grows deeper, and one can experience a burning desire to do the will of God and please Him. When I was a teenager something very powerful happened to me. I attended a wake and the mother's daughter had just died. She was only fourteen years old. The mother was crushed. She had expectations for her daughter and was hoping she would be a gymnast someday. Now she was dead. This dream for her was gone. I saw the anguish of this mother's grief, and she was inconsolable. It really bothered me, and before I went to bed I started to pray for that woman. God revealed to me that we are His children, and He has expectations for us. There is a purpose and a plan for our lives. We have the gift of free will to choose to follow God's plan or not. After seeing this mother's grief and pain it made me realize that God could be hurt and disappointed if we don't follow His plan or have a relationship with Him. It horrified me to think of hurting God like that. It could be a spiritual death being separated from Him and not doing His will in our lives. It opened my eyes to pray every day, "Dear God, help me to want what You want." Then when things happen that I did not plan that way then I say to God, "Truly this must have been Your will because I could have never thought of that."

Other attitudes of the heart develop like trust in God, total dependence on God, being humble, denying one's self, seeking first the kingdom of God, seeking God's perspective in every circumstance, holy and Godly living, and striving to grow in the virtues in order to be like Jesus.

The Journey

One day God revealed to me this example of what our spiritual journey with Him is all about. Let us examine for example a pitcher of ice water. The ice water is in the pitcher filled with ice cubes. The ice cubes are in the form of a solid; the substance is called water. Water is present inside the pitcher and is in the form of a liquid substance. Man is created in the image of God but is not God. Ice cubes and water are the same substance in different forms. As we embark on this spiritual journey in our lives, we gradually melt, die to self, and become water. The final goal is to have union with God and become the water. However, there is a whole process to this that takes a lifetime to achieve. It involves trusting, letting go, and surrendering to God. Events occur in our lives, and we are supposed to grow. Difficulties, hardships, struggles, death of loved ones, loss of jobs, crises develop in our lives. Each day is supposed to prepare us to be closer to God. In each adversity, we are tested. The questions in the testing process include the following: How much do you love Me? How much do you trust Me? Will you let go and surrender to My will? Jesus's life mission was to do the will of the Father. God gave us his perfect Son to die for us to teach us to do the same thing in our lives. A change into Jesus's life is an example to us on how we are supposed to live our lives. He was like us in all things except sin. Jesus life was a journey of trusting His Father, letting go, and surrendering. He taught us the Our Father as an example of how to pray and communicate with God. The same way the ice cubes are transformed into water, our souls are supposed to be transformed. When we pray and place ourselves in the presence of God, we are going to be transformed physically, mentally, spiritually, emotionally, and psychologically. In the final journey when we die, we will become one with God in the same way the ice is melted in the water pitcher. God and soul will be united in heaven for eternity.

Experience God's Presence

When we speak of God's presence, there are four ways to think of God's presence: Universal Presence means God is omnipresent; He is everywhere and anywhere at the same time. Psalm 139:7 explains it as "Where can I go from your Spirit?"

Indwelling Presence is when Christ came into us through the Spirit and dwells in us now. Romans 8:9–11 says, "Not of flesh…but Spirit…if He is in you…" Enabling Presence is when sin can block the effectiveness of a believer. While not keeping him from heaven, sin "short circuits" God's power flowing in and through us. David knew that and so did Paul. In Romans 6–8, "Sin shall not have dominion over me, I'm free."

Manifest Presence is the fourth type. Manifest means "apparent to the senses or the mind; obvious or to show plainly."

A.W. Tozer expresses it so well in his book *The Knowledge of the Holy*. "It remains only for us to learn to realize this presence in conscious experience" (Harper Collins Publishers, New York, NY 1961). Dr. Allan Fleece sums up the testimony of others when he says, "The knowledge that God is present is blessed, but to feel His presence is nothing less than happiness." Tozer addresses it again in *The Pursuit of God:* "God wills that we should push on into His presence and live our whole life there. It is more than a doctrine to be held; it is a life to be enjoyed every moment of every day." The presence of God is the central fact of Christianity. God Himself is waiting for His redeemed children to be pushed into conscious awareness of His presence. The Christian's privilege is present realization. One cannot experience this manifest presence realization while living in sin or disobedience (2006, First WingSpread Publishers Edition, USA). An example of this is in Psalm 51:10–13 when David fell into sin with Bathsheba. David cried out to God, "Create in me a clean heart, O God, and renew a steadfast spirit within me. Do not cast me away from Your Presence, and do not take Your Holy Spirit from me." Psalm 51:12 says that we need to be alert to His prompting. "Restore to me the joy of Your salvation, and sustain me with a willing spirit. Make me willing to obey You." One of the precious "fruits of the Spirit" is self-control. David lost it when he saw Bathsheba bathing that day, but he repented and asked God to restore it once again. "Self-control is simply the instant obedience to the initial promptings of the Holy Spirit. It is a character quality that every believer needs to cultivate by walking in the Spirit. There is no joy without a willingness to do God's will. When we let the old man, the flesh, take over our lives, hearts, and minds, we can say and do things we would have thought impossible." (Life Application Study Bible, New International Version) Psalm 51:13 speaks about the anointing of His power. "Then I will teach transgressors your ways, and sinners will be converted to You." Listen! To live a life of power and demonstration of the Holy Spirit, we must be clean. David realized that his effectiveness in ministry depended on his spiritual condition and restoration. "Then I will teach sinners, and they will be saved." The power is rooted in the anointing, and the anointing is rooted in holiness.

One's life must be clean; "Not by (my) might, not by (my) power, not by personality, not by mind over matter, but by God's Spirit (Zechariah 4:6, New International Version)." One can cherish the anointing. One must realize the need for the power of the Holy Spirit to fill, control, guide, and guard us consciously, continually, and conspicuously. Paul says it all in 2 Corinthians 3:5, "Not that we are adequate in ourselves to consider anything as coming from ourselves, but our adequacy is from God, our only power and success comes from the Lord."

A crisis in one's life is an opportunity for God's blessings. I never knew that Hurricane Sandy would have been such a life-changing experience for me. I experienced God's presence in so many different ways.

I found God in the many faces and people who helped me—my father, my church friends, people I worked with, and the many different organizations, Siller Foundation and Rapid Repair. Groups of young adults who were off from college, they volunteered their time to help remove debris from the house. They helped to do whatever they could to improve the situation. In New York on Staten Island, the community pulled together. I was deeply touched by seeing God in the body of Christ corporately, on a community level. Churches and pastors from all denominations came to my house, spoke to me, and were willing to help me. The sisters that taught me in school were there for me. Personal friends of mine were supportive and expressed their outpouring of love and concern.

My relationships with others and God grew closer. I was still loved in the midst of my mess and when I had nothing to give to anyone and all I could do was receive. All my life I worked hard and never took anything from anyone. This crisis taught me how to receive. It humbled me. Faith in God was what remained for me. As I saw house after house destroyed on my block and all over and garbage being pulled to curbside different thoughts entered my head. At first, it dawned on me where were they going to put all the debris, the stench of it all, and that each one of us has our own garbage. When the garbage was all piled up collectively house after house, it was a moment of revelation for me. We are all human beings that are blessed and broken with all our mess and garbage. We also contain beauty and goodness inside us also. Yet I held onto the idea that our garbage is recyclable. Garbage can be transformed just like the way we plant a garden or the way a farmer grows crops. Fertilizer and horse manure are used to grow delicious vegetables and flowers. The irony and mystery to how this happens. I tried to wrap my head around this thought and hold onto it. Something beautiful will come out of this.

After the garbage was taken out and removed with my material belongings that were lost and destroyed, I felt God showing me some of the garbage I had within myself. I was forced to face my shadow side of myself. My heart was broken; I felt like I was going through what Job went through or Jonah in the Old Testament.

Jonah was sent to Nineveh by God; he did not want to go there. It was a new place for him. It reminded me of the voice of change and crisis that stirred up in my life. My safe world, my house, destroyed, having to start over, a call to newness and change. What was God doing to me? How could He allow this? What was I going to do? How will something beautiful come out of this?

In the story of Jonah, he resisted this call to go to Nineveh; he ran away onto a ship. God was represented in the story as the hurling winds. In the same way, crisis winds often grow more turbulent when we resist the voice of the soul. The difficulty then becomes a full-blown crisis.

As the storm grew worse Jonah hid in the bottom of the ship. Jonah was afraid that everyone would perish; he surrendered to the experience. He came out of hiding and let go; he allowed himself to be cast into the sea. This is the moment of descent into one's inner depths. In this act, Jonah completed the separation and entered the phase of transformation.

As Jonah was swallowed up in the belly of the whale, Jonah entered the cocoon, the dark womb in the sea where his metamorphosis happened. Here we allow ourselves to be digested. In science, to be digested means to be changed in substance. In this process, all we can do is call on God and wait. That is what I did. I waited on God, letting go, descending into the depths of my soul, listening, opening myself up to change, and prayed more, like Jonah's prayer, "I called to the Lord, out of my distress and He answered me, out of the belly of Sheol I cried and thou didst hear my voice." For thou didst cast me into the deep, into the heart of the seas, the waters closed in over me, the deep was round about me. (Jonah 2:2–3, 5)

Waiting is allowing holy waters to close over you. It means having the deep round about you. It is like taking the night sea journey. It is a process that a person goes inward to be born again. We do not cross over into the sphere of rebirth by power, only by descent, by being swallowed.

Emergence begins after Jonah stayed three days and nights inside the belly of the whale in complete darkness and unknowing, waiting. Then he was released from the fish and sent to Nineveh. He emerged as a new person on the shore line of Nineveh. He has come upon the new horizon inside himself. I closed the Bible and realized this was all happening to me. Like Jonah, I had been lifted into the windy spaces of my own soul. For the first time since it all began, I felt myself relax into the storm. I was not so afraid of it now. God's presence was round about me. A moment of truth was revealed to me. We can endure, transcend, and transform the crisis when we see the meaning and mystery of it (reference used: *When the Heart Waits* by Sue Monk Kidd).

There is no greater joy than when a soul is touched by God. God is present inside our own hearts. There is a still point within us. It represents the center, the quiet core where God's spirit dwells in us (1Cor. 3–16). God lives and moves and has being (2 Cor.3:16). In the innermost center of our being, a place where we are deeply and profoundly known and loved by God is the presence in our midst. It is a love meeting an embrace. Hildegard wrote, "God hugs you. You are encircled by the arms of the mystery of God."

In this place, man will see the image of the divine nature in his own beauty. Wherever God is found that is where heaven is. Heaven is union. The glory of God is the manifestation and revelation of His love. Heaven and earth are full of God's glory. We become conscious of the oneness of everything—

one in the all and all in the one. It is collective communion and contemplative fellowship—a peaceful nothingness. God is found in our hearts, and we find ourselves in God.

"I am who I am" (Exodus 3:14).

We are God's offspring. We have God's DNA. Because God lives inside each person, we are to love each person. When we love each other we can see the face of God in them. When they love us, the love and presence of God is experienced, reflected back to us, and mirrored through them.

There is something that I learned that impacted me. Each one of us is a sacrament. A sacrament is an outward sign of God's love instituted by God to give grace. There are seven sacraments in the church. For example, in the sacrament of matrimony, God and man become one. They each agree to marry one another. Their union can be compared to an image of a triangle. God is at the top of the triangle, man is at one base, and woman at the other base. They marry the person and God together. They are supposed to help each other as married partners fulfill God's plan in their lives. They become one. The explosion and union of their love produces the offspring. Just like the explosion of love with the Father and Son produced the Holy Spirit, Godhead three in one.

Jesus gives His body and blood to us in the sacrament of Eucharist. He gives Himself to us personally and corporately as the Body of Christ. Jesus is alive in our hearts, his love and presence. He chose to come to us in the form of bread and wine to be with us everyday. The mass is the remembrance that

He gives Himself to us, and we have an opportunity to have mass every day, not just on Sundays, to receive communion and be in communion with our God every day.

It also extends into our everyday life. For me, I never really understood why I would never want to miss a meal. It is not so much about eating for the sake of eating. It is really about the need for intimacy—to be with the people we love and sharing a meal with them like breaking bread, which we do at mass. Every meal is like a mini Eucharist. It is a celebration of being with the ones you love. It is experiencing God's presence through them. We are signs of God's living presence.

In everyday life experiences, in a simple meal, a sunset, scenes in nature, a beautiful song, seeing a flower, a bird, full moon, throwing out the garbage, doing laundry, and gardening. God is present everywhere. Heaven and earth are full of God's glory every day here and now. This is one of the secrets of the soul. The present moment becomes communion bread that is broken to reveal the presence of Christ. God is everywhere. To take each day as a gift and discover where we will find God next, every day becomes an adventure. I have developed a new spring in my step, a greater appreciation for everything I have—seeing same old things in new ways, having more awareness of God inside me and around me, paying more attention to detail and a sense of feeling more alive. I am able to see more how my life is not just about me and that I am fully connected to God and others and connected to something much greater than myself.

Life is more abundant and I am able to live life more fully now experiencing God's presence.

A picture says a thousand words. Each picture I photographed tells a story; it was taken in a different country and location where I traveled. Some are pictures of the USA, Hawaii, Alaska, California, Greece, Italy, Costa Rica, and Europe. Each picture is a scene from nature. We see God's personality, His character, and a glimpse of God's glory. We experience His presence. Anything that someone creates says a lot about that person. Nature reflects God. Look at the colors; Heaven and Earth are full of God's glory. Enjoy each picture.

Experience God's Presence

Melissa Lanza

Experience God's Presence

Melissa Lanza

Experience God's Presence

Experience God's Presence

Experience God's Presence

Melissa Lanza

Experience God's Presence

Melissa Lanza

Experience God's Presence

Melissa Lanza

Experience God's Presence

Melissa Lanza

Experience God's Presence

Melissa Lanza

Melissa Lanza

Experience God's Presence

Melissa Lanza

Melissa Lanza

Experience God's Presence

Melissa Lanza

Experience God's Presence

Melissa Lanza

Experience God's Presence

Experience God's Presence

Melissa Lanza

Experience God's Presence

Melissa Lanza

Experience God's Presence

Melissa Lanza

Experience God's Presence

Melissa Lanza

Experience God's Presence

Melissa Lanza

Experience God's Presence

Melissa Lanza

Experience God's Presence

In My Presence

The Secret Place of His Presence

In this chapter it is important to realize that there is a parallel when we relate to God that is manifested in human relationships. For example, we are mother, daughter, sister, aunt, cousin, friend, lover, wife, or spouse in our relationships with human beings. Men are husbands, fathers, sons, uncles, friend, lover, and spouse in our relationships with others. There are different ways one can relate to God in anyone of those relationships as described above. However, in this chapter the focus will be God relating to us as brides. It will be explained from one of the books in the Bible, the Song of Songs.

Once a soul expresses a deep hunger for intimacy with God—and please note God puts that desire in us when we were created. We, with our free will, have to choose to want God or not. Psalm 42 states, "As the deer pants for streams of water, so my soul pants for you, O God. My soul thirsts for God, for the living God. Where can I go and meet with God?" Did you know that the word *pant* means to yearn eagerly, more than just breathing rapidly. Do you yearn eagerly for God? Are you truly thirsting after the living God? The second verse found in Psalm 84 describes an intense longing for God's presence. "My soul longs, yes, even faints for the courts of the Lord; my heart and my flesh cry out for the living God."

The Father has created a holy and intimate place inside of us (in the spirit) that the world cannot penetrate called the secret place of His presence. It is reserved for all true believers in Jesus Christ. It is a place of freedom, where our love for Jesus can intensify, both in intimacy and in overflowing, life-giving joy. We need to ask God like the prophet Isaiah did in Isaiah 64: 1–2. The prophet said, "Oh, that You would rend the heavens! That You would come down! That the mountains might shake at Your presence. Yes! Oh God, tear open the heavens and come down! Isn't that what we all want? That the nations may tremble in the presence of God." The Holy Spirit revealed that when we really want Him to tear open the heavens and come down, then at that critical point, He will be released to surprise us with something incredible that we have not been seeking after. Today, people want what the presence of God will bring. They want the benefits and the blessing that comes with God's increased presence in their life, and they pursue Him because they know that the blessing is in the secret place. However, they are not hungry for God only; rather they are hungry for the fruit, the results of what comes from spending time with God in the secret place. Yes, there are many blessings in that place. However, we will only be permitted to see the face of God and receive His kiss of love when we desire Him alone. His kiss is meant for you. God wants you to see His face. In the Song of Songs 1:2–4 states, "Let him kiss me with the kisses of his mouth—for your love is better than wine. Because of the fragrance of your good ointments.

"Your name is ointment poured forth; therefore the virgins love you. Draw me away. We will run after you. The king has brought me into his chambers. We will be glad and rejoice in you. We will remember your love more than wine. Rightly do they love you." The passage is full of intimacy. The young Shulammite bride is speaking, "Let him kiss me with the kisses of his mouth—for your love is better than wine…Draw me away! We will run after you." This young bride is hungry for intimacy, and she is responding to the king's invitation to love and be loved. And then, "The king has brought me into his chambers." Likewise, God is inviting us, His bride, to love Him and be loved by Him. He is the initiator. Without Him we can do nothing. Jesus said, "You did not choose Me, but I chose you" (John 15:16).

"For your love is better than wine." Do you know what this means? Influence. It is like what the Shulammite bride is saying, "There is something in my heart that realizes in order for me to impact the world, and in order for me to love God I need God to kiss me; I need God to quicken me; I need God to draw me; I need God to initiate. I need the wine of God, because if I don't come under the influence of His affection, or unless God's love, like wine, influences me, I can't love Him. I can't even enter the secret place without the wine and the influence of God's affection ravishing my heart to pursue Him." Our cry needs to be "Fill me with Your love and Your wine. Influence me, Oh God. Draw me away." This is the hunger. This is where we abandon ourselves in surrender to pursue God. The intensity of our desire for God goes hand and hand with our passionate pursuit of Him in prayer. Our hunger and the passionate pursuit of God in prayer will cause God to bring us into His chambers. "The king has brought me into His chambers." Isn't this what we all want? It is like each one of us saying, "I want to be with You, Jesus, in the intimate bridal chambers. I want to behold Your beautiful face, and I want to receive Your kiss of love." The bride needs to make herself ready. We need to separate ourselves from carnal mindsets that seek materialism and living for self. Jesus said, "We are not of this world, but I chose you out of the world…" (John 15:19). In Psalm 45:10–11, it speaks about the glories of the Messiah and His bride. "Listen, O daughter, consider and incline your ear; forget your own people also, and your father's house; so the King will greatly desire your beauty; because He is your Lord, worship Him." In the context of the culture in biblical times, a bride often came to her fiancé from a different country. She was advised to forget her own people and her father's house because she would be living in a whole new culture, a brand new world. She needed to let go of the past and embrace her new future. Likewise, we need to separate ourselves from our old way of life when we walked in darkness before we made a decision to follow Jesus Christ. (Col.1:13–14). God is calling us to be consecrated and set apart unto Him; a bride making herself ready. Then the King will desire your beauty; because He is your Lord, bow down to Him (v.11). Do you realize that God sees beauty in you? Holiness, consecration, and abandonment are really precious to Him. Do you want the King to greatly desire your beauty? Psalm 45 continues with "And the daughter of Tyre, she will come with a gift; the rich among the people will seek your favor." Tyre was a wealthy city. Talk about the wealth of the nations. People in the world will see Jesus Christ in us and see the beauty of the Lord, and they will be compelled to bring us the choicest gifts. They will want to come and give a gift to you. There is a preparation taking place in the spirit and the bride is making herself ready to be married to the King. There will be gladness and great joy (Fresh Fire Ministries 1999–2005).

She, the bride, shall be brought to the King in multi-colored robes; the virgins, her companions who follow her, shall be brought to Jesus. With gladness and rejoicing, they shall be brought; they shall enter the King's palace. What happens in the King's palace, or bridal chamber, the sons of Korah do not reveal. The palace doors are closed for the sake of privacy because the intimacy of the secret place cannot be gazed upon by the world. Nothing profane can enter in.

The Shulammite bride in the Song of Songs is eventually transformed into a mature bride, who is seen leaning upon her beloved as they come out of the wilderness together. She is changed by the rapture of love. *Rapture*, according to *Webster's Dictionary*, is the state of being carried away with joy, love, and ecstasy. What is the rapture of love? It is a joyful, passionate love created and reserved (set apart) by God for those believers who are madly in love with Jesus Christ and for those who are joined to Him in intimacy. The Father has created a private place where our love for Jesus can intensify both in intimacy and in overflowing, life-giving joy. Isn't that the perfect place to experience the rapture of love? When our love life with God matures, He is mindful of the multitudes of people who are lost and dying. They need to be reached with the Gospel by Christians whose hearts are aflame with God's burning love. "Set me as a seal upon your heart, as a seal upon your arm; for love is as strong as death, jealousy as cruel as the grave; its flames are flames of fire a most vehement flame" (Song of Songs v.6). Love—its flames are flames of fire! A most severe flame! Friends! God's fiery seal of supernatural love comes upon our hearts to empower us to love a lost world with the very love that Jesus has. It is a mature, fiery, passionate love, full of flames of fire. After all, Jesus came and set the world on fire with His love. As the relationship with God intensifies, God shares with a soul the multitudes of people who are lost and dying. He shows how Christ has nobody now on earth but you. You are His eyes, His hands, and His voice to reach out to others. When this is done for others, we are serving Him.

Ministering to the Lord

Ministry to the Lord is a calling. The book of Acts 13:2–4 states, "While they were worshipping the Lord and fasting, the Holy Spirit said, 'Set apart for me Barnabas and Saul for the work to which I have called them.'" Another example of ministering to the Lord is in the book of Luke 10:38–41:

> Jesus visited Mary and Martha. As Jesus and His disciples were on their way, He came to a village where a woman named Martha opened her home to Him. She had a sister called Mary, who sat at the Lord's feet listening to what He said. But Martha was distracted

by all the preparations that had to be made. She came to Him and asked. "Lord, don't you care that my sister has left me to do the work by myself? Tell her to help me." "Martha, Martha," the Lord answered. "You are worried and upset about many things, but only one thing is needed. Mary has chosen what is better, and it will not be taken away from her."

Mary was able to sit, listen, wait, and be in His presence. It is the prayer of letting Jesus be. God's good pleasure is all that matters. The goal is to just be with each other. It appeared to Martha and to the rest of the world a waste of time because certain tasks were not getting done. The house was not being cleaned up, and the dirty dishes were still in the sink.

Ministering to the Lord involves praise—to praise what God has done and is doing. The Bible states, "He sets up His throne room among the praises of His people." Worship who God is. It involves engaging in the Spirit of the Lord and experiencing the manifest presence of the Lord. We can feel the glory of God. Communion, intimacy, what God wants, what is mine is His and His glory, His grace, His love become mine. "I fell at His feet like a dead man" (Revelation 7:15), the Scripture describes it in the book of Matthew 25:31: "When the Son of Man comes in His glory, and all the angels with him, he will sit on His throne in heavenly glory." Another example can be found in Revelation 4:10: "The twenty-four elders fall down before Him who sits on the throne and worship Him who loves forever and ever. They lay their crowns before the throne and say, 'You are worthy, our Lord and God, to receive glory, honor and power, for you created all things, and by your will they were created and have their being.'" In Revelation 7:11, "All the angels were standing around the throne and around the elders and the four living creatures. They fell down on their faces before the throne and worshipped God saying, 'Amen! Praise and glory, wisdom, thanks, honor, power and strength be to our God for ever and ever. Amen!'"

Revelation 7:15 illustrates an example of ministering to the Lord. It states, "They are before the throne of God and serve him day and night in His temple; and He who sits on throne will spread His tent over them. Never again will they hunger, never again will they thirst. The sun will not beat upon them, or any scorching heat. For the Lamb at the center of the throne will be their shepherd; He will lead them to springs of living water. God will wipe away every tear from their eyes." When should one minister to the Lord? The hour is now. John 4:23 states, "Yet a time is coming and has now come when true worshipers will worship the Father in spirit and truth, for they are the kind of worshipers the Father seeks. God is spirit and His worshipers must worship in spirit and in truth."

Why minister to the Lord? Because God is seeking worshipers and by ministering to the Lord, one learns how to minister to others and the Holy Spirit speaks. This is where the hearts engage in contemplative prayer—the art of being in communion. The soul learns how to sit at the feet of Jesus and be in His presence. The hearts are joined in intimacy. As a result of this union, the soul is better able to serve God and others in ministry. The art of serving is a direct experience of the overflow of this union of love. This deep encounter explains what Jesus taught about how He came to set the world on fire. His life was constantly pointing to the love of His Father. He was only able to bring this to the world, expressing love through action after He had experienced firsthand the love He experienced from His Father. Ministry to the Lord is contemplative prayer and being with Jesus, sitting at His feet. Mary had done this in the scriptures, and she was told she had chosen the better part.

Preserving Our Faith

How to Protect Yourself from Evil

Faith is a gift from God. It needs to be nurtured and preserved. How does one protect this?

In the book of Ephesians 6:11–18, scripture states,

> Put on the full armor of God so that you can take your stand against the devil's schemes. For our struggle is not against flesh and blood, but against the rulers, against the authorities, against the powers of this dark world and against the spiritual forces of evil in the heavenly realms. Put on the full armor of God, so that

when the day of evil comes, you may be able to stand your ground. After you have done everything to stand; then stand firm with the belt of truth buckled around your waist, with the breastplate of righteousness in place, and with your feet fitted with the readiness that comes from the gospel of peace. Take up the shield of faith, with which you can extinguish all the flaming arrows of the evil one. Take the helmet of salvation and the sword of the Spirit, which is the word of God. Pray in the spirit on all occasions with all kinds of prayers and requests. With this in mind, be alert and always keep on praying. There is an invisible world as real as the visible world.

The book of Daniel 10:10–21 gives a glimpse of the invisible world and the visible world. "A hand touched me and sent me trembling on my hands and knees. He said, 'Daniel, you who are highly esteemed, consider carefully the words I am about to speak to you, and stand up, for I have now been sent to you.' When he said this to me, I stood up trembling. Then he continued, 'Do not be afraid, Daniel. Since the first day that you set your mind to gain understanding and to humble yourself before your God, your words were heard, and I have come in response to them. But the prince of the Persian kingdom resisted me twenty-one days. Then Michael, one of the chief princes, came to help me, because I was detained there with the king of Persia. Now I have come to explain to you what will happen to your people in the future, for the vision concerns a time yet to come.' While he was saying this to me, I bowed with my face toward the ground and was speechless. Then one who looked like a man touched my lips and I opened my mouth and began to speak. I said to the one standing before me, 'I am overcome with anguish because of the vision, my lord, and I am helpless.' The one who looked like a man touched me and gave me strength. 'Do not be afraid, O man highly esteemed,' he said. 'Peace! Be strong now, be strong.' When he spoke to me, I was strengthened and said, 'Speak, my lord, since you have given me strength.' He said, 'Do you know why I have come to you? Soon I will return to fight against the prince of Persia, and when I go, the prince of Greece will come; but first I will tell you what is written in the book of truth.'"

Scripture explains in the book of Ephesians 6:12 about the real invisible world. It states that our struggle is not against flesh and blood but against rulers, against the authorities, against the powers of this dark world, and against the spiritual forces of evil in the heavenly realms. We learn from this scripture, as described above, that our foe is formidable, and his goal is to destroy us and discredit Christ. We must respect but not fear him; and we must be aware of his methods, but not overly preoccupied with them. As believers, we do not fight for victory, we fight from victory.

It is important to realize that Satan is out to discourage, deceive, divide, and destroy God's people and program. Believers are commanded to equip, to prepare, and to know his schemes and strategies. There are four keys to spiritual victory. We must become aware of the invisible war. We must learn to appropriate God's protection for daily living. We must engage the enemy with supernatural weapons and utilize God's means of deliverance. When spiritually attacked, stand firm and put on the full armor of God. Claim the blood of Jesus over you and state in the name of Jesus, "Get behind me, Satan." Be aware of the lies Satan uses to deceive us. Some of the lies are as follows: Take care of yourself first and foremost because nobody else will. The Bible was written centuries ago, it is not relevant today. Truth is relative, what is true for you may not be true for others. The Bible can't be true; it was written in the same way the game of telephone is played. In the end, the message is distorted, and the truth is lost. If God were all loving, He would not let bad things happen to good people. I am going to stand up for my rights regardless of the consequences. These are only some of the temptations and deceit of Satan. There are many more.

It is encouraging to know that Satan was defeated at Calvary. Satan's penalty was paid for all time and all people. Sin's power was broken. Here are some questions we can ask ourselves as we prepare for victory: Where am I deceived? How about my heart, is it right with God? Have I hurt anyone that I need to make peace with? Learn to protect your faith and guard your hearts for the devil is prowling like a roaring lion looking for someone to devour.

Some techniques for spiritual victory is having the awareness of the struggle between good and evil. Temptations develop daily to do evil and to give in to ungodly behavior and sin.

It is helpful to know oneself. The gift of self-knowledge is so important. When we know who we are as persons, we are able to identify our strengths and weaknesses. We can identify weaknesses and be aware of them. It is very important to identify them early on before one falls into sin. As we grow in self-knowledge, we can identify patterns and work through it when we are tempted. We must realize that the foe is formidable, and Satan's goal is to destroy us and discredit Christ. We must respect, but not fear him and become aware of his methods, but not overly preoccupied with them.

Rewards

The rewards are priceless. A person's soul will develop the fruits or gifts of the Holy Spirit and become transformed. It is a process similar to a person sitting in the sun every day. Gradually, a person will get a tan, and their skin will get darker. Internally, our souls will change and be more pleasing to God. We will start to die to self and be transformed. We will be on our way to heaven.

All members of the church, Christ's body, are gifted by the presence of the Holy Spirit. Each person's experience of the Holy Spirit is for the good of the body. That is why we need each other. Without a healthy and functioning body, a church will miss out on the good God provides for it.

In 1 Corinthians 12:4, it states that there are different kinds of gifts but the same Spirit. There are different kinds of service but the same Lord. There are different kinds of working but the same God works in all men. The manifestation of the Spirit is given for the common good. To one there is given, through the Spirit, the message of wisdom; to another the message of knowledge by means of the same Spirit. Other gifts include faith, gifts of healing, miraculous powers, prophecy, and distinguishing between spirits. To another is speaking in different kinds of tongues and the interpretation of tongues. All of these are the works of one and the same Spirit, and he gives them to each one, just as he determines. The body is a unit even though it is made up of many parts; though the parts are many they form one body. So it is with Christ for we were all baptized by one Spirit into one body whether Jews or Greeks, slave or free. We were all given the one Spirit to drink. God has arranged the parts in the body just as He wanted them to be. You are the body of Christ, and each one of you is part of it. One part is not better than the other. In the church, God has appointed first the apostles; second, prophets; third, teachers; then workers of miracles—those with the gifts of healing and able to help others, gifts of administration, and those speaking in different tongues. The rewards of being in the body of Christ enable a person to develop the gifts that God gave them and to serve God and others in their communities and in the world.

In Luke 6:40, the promise in the scripture is to be like Jesus. The book of Galatians 5:22-25, speaks about the fruits of the spirit: love, joy, peace, patience, kindness, goodness, faithfulness, gentleness, and self control. As a soul progresses and grows in relationship with God, it will grow and develop these fruits and virtues. This is one of the rewards that one obtains. What does God say about what these gifts are in the scriptures? Of course, one obtains these gifts by being in God's presence daily as this book has described in detail.

An example of love, which is the fruit or gift of the Holy Spirit, is cited in John 15:13. It states, "My command is this: Love each other as I have loved you. Greater love has no one than this that he lay down his life for his friends." Jesus lived this out by dying on the cross for us.

The gift of joy is described in John 15:11 and in Hebrews 12:2. It states, "I have told you this so that my joy may be in you and that your joy may be complete." Let us fix our eyes on Jesus, the author and perfecter of our faith, who for the joy set before him endured the cross, scorning its shame, and sat down at the right hand of the throne of God. *Joy* is described as gladness, happiness, and rejoicing.

Peace is described in John 14:27: "Peace I leave with you, my peace I give you. I do not give to you as the world gives. Do not let your hearts be troubled and do not be afraid." Peace is also mentioned in John 16:33: "I have told you these things so that in me you may have peace. In this world you will have trouble. But take heart I have overcome the world." Lastly, in John 20:19–26, Jesus appeared to His disciples and stated, "Peace be with you, as the Father has sent me, I am sending you." Then He breathed on them and said, "Receive the Holy Spirit. If you forgive anyone his sins, they are forgiven; if you do not forgive them, they are not forgiven." Jesus also appeared to Thomas through locked doors and stated, "Peace be with you." Then He stated to Thomas, "Put your finger here, see my hands. Reach out your hand and put it into my side. Stop doubting and believe." *Peace* is defined as a state of tranquility, a calm and quiet according to *Webster's Dictionary*. It is a great gift of the Holy Spirit to have.

The gift of patience is referenced in Luke 15:11–32 in the story of the prodigal son. It portrays the image of a patient father waiting for his son to return home with him. According to *Webster's Dictionary*, *patience* means to have calm endurance without compliance or forbearance.

Kindness is another gift of the Holy Spirit found in Romans 11:22, Matthew 19:13–15, Jonah 4:2 and Ephesians 2:4–10. These references describe the love Christ has for us. This love is very rich in mercy, making us alive in Christ even when we were dead in transgressions. It has been by grace that you have been saved. God raised us up with Christ and seated us with him in the heavenly realms in Christ Jesus, in order that in the coming ages he might show the incomparable riches of his grace, expressed in his kindness to us in Christ Jesus. *Kindness,* as defined by *Webster,* is the quality of being benevolent and well-disposed.

Goodness is mentioned in Luke 18:1–19. A certain ruler asked Jesus, "Good teacher, what must I do to inherit eternal life?" Jesus answered, "Why do you call me good? No one is good except God alone." Ephesians 5:9 states, "Live as children of light (for the fruit of the light consists in all goodness, righteousness and truth) and find out what pleases the Lord." Webster defines *goodness* as pleasing, considerable, and benevolent in unquestionable standing.

Faithfulness is another fruit of the spirit. In Luke 22:39–46, Jesus was tested in the garden of Gethsemane, yet Jesus remained faithful to His Father. Jesus said, "Father, if you are willing take this cup from me, yet not my will but your will be done. Being in anguish, Jesus prayed more earnestly, and His sweat was like drops of blood falling to the ground. *Faithfulness*, as described by Webster, means trusting, loyal, trustworthy, true, and accurate.

Gentleness is another fruit of the Holy Spirit. Luke 22:47–53 tells the story of Jesus's arrest. Jesus was questioned by His followers, "Should we strike with our swords?" One of them struck the servant of the high priest and cut off his ear. Jesus answered, "No more of this!" Jesus touched the man's ear and healed him. Matthew 5:5 says, "Blessed are the meek for they will inherit the earth." *Gentleness*, as described by Webster, is wellborn, mild, kindly, docile, soft, soothing, and tame.

Self-control is the ninth fruit of the Holy Spirit. Luke 4:1–13 describes the temptation of Jesus in the desert for forty days and nights. Jesus was tempted in all ways but managed to keep his self-control. Another example is in Matthew 26:47–56 when Jesus was arrested, and He was having excellent self-control. He did not succumb to the violence that occurred when the servant of the high priest had his ear cut off. Jesus remained calm and collected. Webster defined *self-control* as control of oneself and one's passions.

    The rewards of being in God's presence are things that only God can do. Once God draws people to Himself, God causes people to seek after Him. This happens because once the soul is touched by God Himself, nothing else satisfies it; and such hunger, desire, and love is created in the soul of the person as the relationship forms. God reveals spiritual truth. God convicts the world of guilt regarding sin. God convicts the world of righteousness. God convicts the world of judgment.

The Call of the Great Commission

Matthew 28:16–20 tells us, "Then the eleven disciples went to Galilee, to the mountain where Jesus told them to go. When they saw Him, they worshipped Him, but some doubted. Then Jesus came to them and said, 'All authority in heaven and on earth has been given to me. Therefore go and make disciples of all nations baptizing them in the name of the Father and of the Son and of the Holy Spirit, and teaching them to obey everything I have commanded you. Surely I am with you always, to the very end of the age.'"

It is time now for you to fill your role and do the will of the Father. Fulfill the role and purpose that your life was created for. God created you for a purpose, the same way Jesus's life had a purpose.

"The water that I gave you to drink will become a spring of water welling up to eternal life and whoever drinks of this water will never thirst again" (John 4:1–42). The water is God and having total union with Him here and in eternal life. Finally, now the ice cubes have melted, we die to self and become immersed in God. What a journey.

As this book described, just take one day at a time and see the fruits of being in God's presence. Seek the call of God *in my presence* for you have chosen the better part. Well done good and faithful servant. May you Experience God's Presence and dwell in the house of the Lord all the days of your life.